JUST ABOUT THE GREATEST EVENT IN BEARTOWN HISTORY!

That's what folks are saying about the classic car show...that is, until valuable vehicles—including Papa's shiny red roadster—mysteriously disappear from the show lot. The Bear Detectives are hot on the trail. But when fresh tracks of some classic car tires lead them straight to Two-Ton Grizzly's auto graveyard, they stop cold. Is Two-Ton the mastermind of the Great Car Robbery...or could it be *the ghost of the auto graveyard?*

BIG CHAPTER BOOKS

The Berenstain Bears and the GHOST OF THE AUTO GRAVEYARD

by the Berenstains

A BIG CHAPTER BOOK™

Random House New York

http://www.randomhouse.com/

Library of Congress Cataloging-in-Publication Data
Berenstain, Stan, 1923–
The Berenstain Bears and the ghost of the auto graveyard /
Stan & Jan Berenstain.
p. cm. — (Big chapter books)
SUMMARY: Thieves strike a classic car show before it opens, causing the inhabitants of Beartown to wonder who or what is behind the crime.
ISBN 0-679-87651-0 (trade) — ISBN 0-679-97651-5 (lib. bdg.)
[1. Automobiles—Fiction. 2. Bears—Fiction.
3. Mystery and detective stories.] I. Berenstain, Jan, 1923—. II. Title.
III. Series: Berenstain, Stan, 1923– Big chapter book.
PZ7.B4483Beffc 1997
[Fic]—dc21 96-52537

Printed in the United States of America 10 9 8 7 6 5 4 3 2 1

BIG CHAPTER BOOKS is a trademark of Berenstain Enterprises, Inc.

Contents

Contents

Chapter 1
A Major Event

"Papa, dear," said Mama Bear, "please put away the morning paper and listen. The cubs are talking about school."

Papa looked up from the newspaper that he had placed beside his bowl of blueberries on the breakfast table. "Cool?" he said. "Then close the window." He went back to his reading.

It happened almost every morning. Mama or the cubs would say something, and Papa, lost in newsprint, would misunderstand. Often he wouldn't hear at all. Reading the morning paper at breakfast was a habit he just couldn't seem to break. Sometimes, though, he found an article that interested everyone. And that's exactly what happened on this particular morning.

"Not *cool*, Papa," said Sister. "*School!*"

Papa looked up again. "School? How did you know I was reading about your school?"

"Reading about our school?" said Brother. "What does it say?"

Papa cleared his throat and read aloud. "'Beartown Mayor Horace J. Honeypot yesterday announced the first annual Beartown Classic Car Show.'"

"What does a car show have to do with school?" asked Sister.

"Hold your horsepower," said Papa. "I'm getting to that." He continued reading: " 'The show will be held for the benefit of Bear Country School and will be sponsored and run by the local PTA. Prizes will be awarded to the three finest classic cars. The mayor said...,' blah, blah, blah. Well, anyway, to put into a few words what it took that old windbag a couple hundred to say: It's going to be a major event, with classic cars brought in from all over Bear Country. It'll be held on the school athletic field this weekend."

"Cool," said Brother.

"Cooler than you think, son," said Papa.

"Why?" asked Brother.

"Because I just happen to be thinking of entering the Bear family car in the show," said Papa with a wink.

"Our red roadster?" Mama scoffed. "Oh, come on, dear. I'll admit it's old. But I'd hardly call it a *classic!*"

Papa turned to look out the kitchen window at his beloved red roadster in the driveway. He smiled. "It sure looks like a classic to me," he said proudly. "What do you think, son?"

Brother seemed to be looking at the roadster, too. But he was really watching the street for Cousin Fred, Lizzy Bruin, and Bonnie Brown. They were due any minute to pick up Brother and Sister so they could all walk to school together, as usual. Today was Monday, and Brother hadn't seen Bonnie since last Wednesday because she'd gone to Big Bear City for a long weekend on a modeling job. He'd missed her a lot.

"Son?" Papa repeated. "What do you think?"

Brother still didn't answer.

"He thinks Bonnie Brown is cute," Sister snickered.

Brother heard Sister because she mentioned Bonnie. "Cut it out!" he snapped.

"Why shouldn't you think Bonnie's cute?" Sister teased. "She's your girlfriend, isn't she?"

"No, she's not," said Brother firmly. "She's just my friend."

"Yeah, sure," said Sister. "And I'm Mayor Horace J. Honeypot."

"Stop arguing, you two," said Papa. "Tell me what's been happening at school lately."

"We already did," said Brother, "but you were reading the newspaper." He jumped up, straining to see far down the road. "Besides, here they come!"

But then Brother's face fell. Coming down the road, with their backpacks slung over their shoulders, were Cousin Fred and Lizzy Bruin. But no Bonnie Brown.

Chapter 2
A Classic

"Where's Bonnie?" asked Brother as the cubs set off for school.

"Don't know," said Cousin Fred. "Maybe she's not back from Big Bear City yet."

"Brother misses his girlfriend," Sister explained.

"I said cut it out, Sis!"

Sister didn't say another word. But Brother was in for more teasing when the cubs joined their friends in the schoolyard to wait for the morning bell to ring.

"What are you looking for?" wondered Babs Bruno. Brother was staring off down the street in the direction of Grizzly Mansion.

"Not what—*who*," said Sister.

"You mean Bonnie?" asked Barry Bruin.

"Bingo," said Sister. She leaned over to Barry and whispered loudly, *"He misses his girlfriend."*

"I heard that!" said Brother. The other cubs snickered. "She's *not* my girlfriend," he protested. "She's my best friend. And that's better than a girlfriend."

"Oh, sure," said Queenie McBear. "And a cheese sandwich is better than an ice cream sandwich."

"Bonnie is *not* a cheese sandwich!" said Brother.

"Then she must be an ice cream sandwich," said Queenie.

"In a shiny wrapper!" added Barry. "Wow! Look at *that!*"

A gleaming silver car had just pulled up at the front gate. Bonnie was in the backseat, and one of Squire Grizzly's chauffeurs was at the wheel.

"It's a beauty!" said Barry, wide-eyed.

Ferdy Factual was polishing his glasses with a monogrammed handkerchief. Now he put them back on, looked at the car, and frowned. "But that's not one of Squire Grizzly's Grizzillac limousines," he said. "What kind of car is it, Barry?"

Ferdy Factual, cub genius, asking Barry Bruin a question? It might have seemed odd if the other cubs hadn't known them both so well. Ferdy was indeed a genius about math, science, geography, and lots of other subjects. But there were a few things he admitted knowing almost nothing about. Cars were one of them. He could describe in great detail the operation of the internal combustion engine under a car's hood. But when it came to recognizing the year and make of the car itself, he was lost.

Barry Bruin, on the other hand, knew a lot about cars. Not because he was a genius.

Far from it. His friends liked to joke that Barry had asked his mom to sew nametags in all his clothes so that if he forgot his name he could look it up. But although he didn't even know what the word "combustion" meant, Barry could recognize the year and make of any car from a hundred yards away. He had spent countless hours making miniature models of classic cars. And he owned the largest collection of classic-car collector's cards in all Bear Country.

"What *is* it?" said Barry in a shocked tone of voice. "You don't recognize *that?*"

"Don't be cute," said Ferdy with a bored yawn. "Just tell us what it is."

"It's a 1927 Bearcedes touring car!" breathed Barry.

"Is it an antique?" asked Lizzy.

Barry laughed. "No, it's a *brand-new* 1927 Bearcedes touring car. Of *course* it's an antique!" He seemed pleased that someone else looked like a dummy for a change.

"It may be an antique," said Cousin Fred, "but it's in beautiful condition."

"Squire Grizzly has a collection of classic cars, and he keeps them all in beautiful condition," said Barry. "I'll bet he's going to enter some of them in the classic car show this weekend."

Bonnie, who had just come skipping up, confirmed what Barry had just said.

"Uncle's going to put the Bearcedes and three other cars in the show," she said. "He wants to win all three prizes, so he's entering four cars just to make sure. One of them is in the shop right now. But it'll be ready in plenty of time."

"What's wrong with it?" asked Brother.

"Not much," said Bonnie. "It needs a tune-up and a new fan belt."

"To qualify for the show," Barry explained, "a car must be authentic *and* in perfect running order."

"Yeah," said Too-Tall Grizzly, who had been listening in with his gang. "That's why there wouldn't even *be* a car show without my dad!"

Too-Tall's father, Two-Ton, owned a business called Parts R Us, on the outskirts of town near Birder's Woods. On his vast lot, among the hulks of wrecked cars and trucks, were piles and piles of used auto parts.

"With all due respect to your father," said Ferdy, "I fail to see what an auto graveyard could possibly have to do with magnificent classic cars."

"Auto graveyard?" growled Too-Tall. "Take that back, you little twerp, or I'll put *you* in the graveyard!"

Quickly, Brother stepped in between Too-Tall and Ferdy. "Easy, big guy," he said. "I don't think Ferdy meant to insult your dad."

With another bored yawn, Ferdy said, "Insulting your father was the furthest thing from my mind. It's just that I can't see what his smelly dump has to do with the noble scientific achievement of the internal combustion engine."

"*Smelly dump?*" roared Too-Tall, balling

up his huge fists. "Lemme at him! I'm gonna combust that little nerd right in the nose!"

Brother moved away as Too-Tall raised a fist at Ferdy.

"Aren't you going to protect Ferdy?" Bonnie said with alarm.

Brother just shrugged. "I already tried," he said. "If Ferdy wants to commit suicide, that's his business."

Fortunately, Queenie stepped in to calm down her on-again, off-again boyfriend. "He didn't mean it," she cooed, taking Too-Tall's arm. "You've got to remember: His IQ may be off the charts, but his SQ is zero."

"SQ?" said Too-Tall, puzzled.

"Sensitivity quotient," said Queenie.

Too-Tall still looked just as puzzled *and* just as angry. But by now Trudy Brunowitz had darted in to pull her genius boyfriend away from danger. The other cubs could hear her lecturing Ferdy about consideration for others. "Even big bullies like Too-Tall have feelings!" she scolded.

Truth was, Too-Tall and Ferdy were both right. Two-Ton's place of business was indeed an auto graveyard and a smelly dump. But it also had a lot to do with keeping Bear Country's classic cars running. At the front entrance was a big sign that said

PARTS R US: IF WE AIN'T GOT IT, WE'LL
GET IT! That pretty much told the story.
There was hardly a classic car anywhere in
Bear Country that didn't have at least one
part supplied by Two-Ton. Squire Grizzly
himself sometimes went looking for parts at

the "auto graveyard." In fact, the 1927 Bearcedes that had just brought Bonnie to school was running on a camshaft that the squire had dug out of one of Two-Ton's wrecks.

Of course, Too-Tall and Ferdy, opposites in so many ways, were exactly alike when it came to arguments. Neither was about to admit that the other might have a point. And though Ferdy was a genius and a nerd, he was no coward. One time he had stood up to Too-Tall when the big guy had gotten all riled up over Queenie making eyes at Ferdy. "If you don't watch out," Too-Tall had snarled, "I'm gonna give you a bloody nose!"

"Oh, yeah?" said Ferdy. "If *you* don't watch out, *I'm* going to give *you* a bloody fist!" Too-Tall got so confused that he forgot he was angry.

This time, however, Too-Tall seemed so angry that the other cubs were afraid he might actually hurt Ferdy. So Queenie and Trudy made sure to keep their stubborn boyfriends occupied until the morning bell rang and everyone filed into school.

Chapter 3
A Not-So-Hidden Treasure

In class that morning, the cubs found out that Mr. Honeycomb, the school principal, had put Teacher Bob in charge of the school's role in the classic car show. Teacher Bob, who liked classic cars himself, was excited. He immediately called an after-school meeting for that very day to recruit cubs for various tasks. He was so excited, in fact, that he couldn't wait until after school. Instead, he held the "after-school" meeting during the day's final school period.

The first thing Teacher Bob did was form a student committee, with Barry Bruin, the car expert, as chairbear. Brother Bear was appointed deputy chairbear. Because of her modeling experience, Bonnie Brown was chosen to pose with her uncle's 1927 Bearcedes touring car for the show poster. Babs Bruno was selected to write press releases and radio promos, which Harry McGill would print out on his computer. And last but not least, Too-Tall and his gang were assigned to direct visitor parking.

As the cubs filed out of the classroom at the final bell, Queenie McBear hurried up to Teacher Bob. "You forgot about me!" she said. "What am *I* in charge of?"

After a moment's thought, Teacher Bob

said, "Er...uh...you're in charge of keeping Too-Tall in line."

As disappointed as Queenie was, that's how thrilled Barry Bruin was. Not only was he the head of a committee for the first time in his life, he was suddenly ten times more popular than he'd ever been. A knot of cubs crowded round him on the front steps of the schoolhouse. Each cub had a family car in mind for him to check out. But it was Brother Bear who got his attention first.

"You should take a look at Papa's red roadster," Brother told Barry. "I think it's pretty old, but I'm not sure it's classic enough for the show."

"Roadster, eh?" said Barry. "Oh, sure. I've seen it around town. Let's go check it out."

So Barry walked home with Brother, Sister, Lizzy, Cousin Fred, and Bonnie Brown.

"Hmm," said Barry when he saw the roadster in the tree house driveway. "I've never really taken a close look at it."

This time he did. He looked it up and down, over and under, and every which way.

"Well?" said Brother. "Is it a classic?"

"Yes" was Barry's answer.

"Yahoo!" cried Sister. "Wait'll Papa hears!"

"What kind of car is it?" asked Cousin Fred.

"It's a 1954 GG roadster," said Barry. "Quite rare."

"What does 'GG' stand for?" asked Bonnie.

"Grizzly Garage," said Barry. "The company went out of business that very same year. In fact, this roadster is the last model GG produced. That makes it very valuable."

Just then Papa Bear came around the tree house from his workshop. "Hi, cubs," he said. "What's up?"

"Papa, do you have any idea what you've got here?" said Sister, gesturing at the car.

"Sure," said Papa. "A 1954 GG roadster."

"You mean, you knew all along?" said Brother, astonished.

"Sure," said Papa, giving his car a friendly pat on the hood. "Gramps bought it

brand-new in '54. He sold it to me when he bought his pickup truck."

"Did you realize it would become a classic when GG went out of business?" asked Fred.

Papa frowned. "Went out of business? GG? When?"

"In 1954!" said Brother. "You've got the last model they ever made!"

Papa's frown turned into a smile. "Well,

what do you know," he said softly. "It must be worth a lot more than I thought. Guess it's good enough for the classic car show, eh?"

"Without a doubt," said Barry. "It'll need some work first, though. Authentic hubcaps and a genuine hood ornament, for example."

"I'll get on it as soon as possible," said Papa.

"Forget the car show, Papa!" said Sister.

"Why?" asked Papa.

"Because this car must be worth a fortune!" said Sister. "You could sell it!"

"Yeah," said Lizzy. "To a collector who wants to put it in the show."

"My uncle, for instance," said Bonnie.

Papa gave Bonnie a very serious look. Then he smiled and started to chuckle.

"What's so funny?" said Sister.

"Now, look, honey," said Papa. "Do you think Squire Grizzly would sell his whole classic car collection to another collector who wanted to put it into the show?"

"Of course not," said Sister. "But what's that got to do with our red roadster?"

Papa gently patted the hood of the car again. "This," he said, "is *my* classic collection. If I sold it to another collector, I'd lose my entire collection."

Most of the cubs shrugged and looked confused. But one of them seemed to understand.

Barry nodded and said, "He has a point, you know."

Chapter 4
The Auto Graveyard

Barry, Lizzy, and Cousin Fred went home, while Bonnie stayed to talk with Brother, Sister, and Papa about the red roadster.

"Maybe my uncle knows a collector who has a GG roadster hood ornament," she told Papa.

"Maybe so," said Papa, "and maybe no. But before I bother the squire with my classic car problems, I want to make a thorough check of our own local treasure trove of car parts."

"You mean Parts R Us?" asked Brother.

"Exactly," said Papa. "Problem is, I'm so

busy with work that it'll be a few days before I can get to it. And the big show is this weekend."

Brother had an idea. "How about if Sister and I go to Parts R Us and check it out?" he suggested.

"That'd be real helpful," said Papa.

But Sister had different ideas. "No way," she said firmly. "I'm not setting foot in that greasy, smelly old dump of an auto graveyard."

"Come on, Sis," said Brother. "It'll do you good to get greasy and smelly for a change."

Sister just shook her head and stubbornly folded her arms.

Papa motioned Brother over and whispered, "I don't think it's the 'greasy' or 'smelly' part that's bothering your sister, son. It's the 'graveyard' part. You know how Sister feels about spooky places."

"But it's not a real graveyard," Brother whispered back. "It's just a bunch of old cars."

"Nevertheless," whispered Papa, "it can be a pretty spooky place. Especially in late afternoon, when the sun is going down and the shadows loom large..."

Brother shivered in spite of himself. But he wasn't going to look chicken like his sister. "What about you, Bonnie?" he said bravely. "You'll come with me, won't you?"

"Sure," said Bonnie. "It's a date."

"Some date," muttered Sister. "Going to a smelly old auto graveyard!"

Papa was too busy that day to give

Brother and Bonnie a ride to Parts R Us. So they walked. Parts R Us was out on the main highway just past Birder's Woods. It was a good half-hour stroll from the Bears' tree house.

By the time Brother and Bonnie got there, the bright afternoon sunshine was already starting to fade. They went straight to Two-Ton Grizzly's office, which was in a huge truck cab resting on piles of railroad ties. Behind the office was the Grizzly family home, an even stranger building. It looked as if it were made of truck bodies welded together. That's because it *was* made of truck bodies welded together. The rumor was that all the furniture in the house had seat belts. The Grizzlys had lived in their weird house for so many years that when they tried moving to an ordinary house, they couldn't get used to it.

Two-Ton looked at Brother and Bonnie with surprise as they climbed into his office. He swung his feet down off his desk. "All right," he said to Brother, "what's that cub of mine done now? So help me, if he's bothered you or your girlfriend..."

Brother blushed. "Bonnie's not my girlfriend," he said. "She's just my friend."

"Whatever," said Two-Ton.

"Anyway, we're not here about Too-Tall,"

Brother explained. "We're looking for a hood ornament for a 1954 GG roadster. Have you got one?"

"If we ain't got it, we'll get it," said Two-Ton, putting his feet back on the desk.

"But have you got it *now*?" asked

Brother. "We need it in time for the big car show. We also need hubcaps."

Two-Ton shrugged his massive shoulders and waved a hand at his windshield window. Through it the cubs could see the vast auto graveyard. "Your guess is as good as mine," he said. "My suggestion is to start at the back and work your way up to the front. That way you'll end up here by closing time—which is six o'clock sharp, by the way. If you get lost, just walk around until you catch sight of the office. That's why I built it on top of railroad ties—to help folks who get lost out there. That, and so I can keep a lookout for parts thieves."

The cubs thanked Two-Ton and walked away from the office, through a forest of wrecked cars and used parts, until they could see a chain-link fence.

"This must be the back," said Brother,

looking around. They were surrounded by heaps of junk. "Let's get to work."

For two solid hours, Brother and Bonnie climbed through wrecked cars and sorted through mounds of parts. It was beginning to get dark when they finally found the hub-caps. A complete set of four, with the GG logo on each. And they were in perfect condition—at least they appeared to be so in what was left of the late afternoon light.

"Fantastic!" said Bonnie. "Do you think they're from a 1954 roadster?"

"We can hope," said Brother.

Bonnie wanted to leave the hubcaps at the office and go home, but Brother insisted they keep looking. "Where there are GG hubcaps," he said, "there just might be a GG hood ornament, too."

After a few more minutes of searching, though, Bonnie had had enough. "Come on, let's go home," she said. "It's getting so dark I can't even tell what these parts are anymore." She held one up. "Is this a hood ornament?"

Brother squinted in the gloom. "Nah," he said. "That's a door handle, I think. Wish we had a flashlight."

Just then a beam of light shone through a pile of truck parts. Heavy footsteps sounded in the dusk.

"*Someone* has a flashlight," whispered Bonnie. *"And here he comes!"*

"Quick, get down!" whispered Brother.

The cubs crouched beside a wrecked pickup truck and shivered with fright as the footsteps and flashlight beam came around the pile of junk.

When the light hit them right in the eyes, they screamed.

"Calm down, cubs," said a gruff voice. "It's just me, Two-Ton. Closin' time."

Brother and Bonnie heaved sighs of relief and fell into each other's arms.

"I thought you two were just friends," chuckled Two-Ton.

"We are," said Brother. "You scared us, that's all."

"Whatever," said Two-Ton. "Come on, let's get back to the office before it gets *really* dark. My night vision stinks. I'm afraid I'll trip over something and break my neck."

But Two-Ton didn't seem to have any trouble seeing in the dark. He moved so quickly among the mountains of wrecks and parts that the cubs could hardly keep up with him.

"Whew!" said Two-Ton when they were safely back in the brightly lit office. "That's better."

"If your night vision is so bad, then how do you catch parts thieves at night?" asked Brother.

"I don't," said Two-Ton. "I leave that to Too-Too and Too-Much. Their night vision is a lot better than mine."

At first it seemed strange to Brother and Bonnie that the biggest, strongest bear in Beartown would leave catching thieves to his wife and daughter. But after a moment's thought, it didn't seem so strange, after all. Two-Ton's wife was small but fierce. And Too-Much, Two-Ton's daughter, worked as a bouncer at a local bar and was one tough cookie.

"Your papa called," Two-Ton told Brother. "He's pretty upset with you cubs for staying out so late. He's on his way over now. It's a good thing you found those hubcaps to soften him up. What's that you've got in your hand, Bonnie?"

"Oh, this?" said Bonnie. "Just a door handle I forgot to throw back."

But as they all looked closer, they saw it wasn't a door handle. It was a hood ornament. With the GG logo on it!

"By golly!" said Two-Ton. "I'll bet that thing was taken off the same car as the hubcaps. When he sees the stuff you found, Papa Bear's gonna stay mad for about one second!"

Chapter 5
Lost and Found

Two-Ton was right. Papa didn't stay angry long when he saw the genuine GG hood ornament and hubcaps that Brother and Bonnie had found. After dropping Bonnie off at Grizzly Mansion, Papa and Brother hurried to Barry Bruin's house to ask the local classic car expert to identify the parts. Barry checked his car books and was able to match the hood ornament with a picture of a 1954 GG roadster. But the hubcaps were a different story. They looked just like the hubcaps from several different makes of GG roadster.

"How can we nail this down?" asked Papa.

Barry shrugged. "I wonder if Grizzly Gramps remembers who sold him the roadster back in '54," he said. "Maybe a former GG dealer could tell if these are '54 hubcaps."

As soon as he and the cubs got home, Papa called Gramps and explained his problem.

Gramps thought for a while. "Nope," he said finally. "I can sort of picture him. But I can't remember the young feller's name." He paused. "Wait a minute. I've got an idea. Don't move. I'll be right over."

Papa, Mama, and the cubs were still debating what Gramps's idea might be when Gramps pulled up in his pickup truck and hurried up the front steps of the tree house.

"Let's have a look at one of those hub-caps," he said eagerly.

"Right over there," said Papa. He had stacked them on a towel in the corner.

Gramps picked up one of the hubcaps and looked it over. "Aha!" he cried. "I knew it!" He held the hubcap up so that the others could see the letters that had been scratched on the inner surface. "There! You see? *GG!*"

Papa, Mama, and the cubs gave each other puzzled looks.

"So a Grizzly Garage hubcap says GG on the inside," said Papa. "So what? It says GG on the outside, too."

"No, no, *no!*" cried Gramps. "Not GG for

'Grizzly Garage'! GG for *'Grizzly Gramps'*! I scratched my initials inside all the hubcaps of my roadster. So if they ever got stolen, the police could tell they were mine!"

It took a moment for what Gramps was saying to sink in.

Finally, Brother said, "You mean, these are the exact same hubcaps that were on our red roadster when you bought it in 1954, Gramps?"

"Yep," said Gramps. "Without a doubt. Same goes for the hood ornament, I expect."

"When were they stolen?" asked Mama.

"In 1955," said Gramps. "Police never caught the thief. What's wrong, Brother? You look kind of funny."

At first Brother didn't realize that Gramps was speaking to him. "Oh," he said,

"I was just thinking about *where* Bonnie and I found the parts..." His voice trailed off.

"Hmm," said Gramps. "You don't mean— Two-Ton Grizzly, a thief? Oh, no. That's ridiculous. Two-Ton is an honest business-bear. Always has been and always will be."

"Gramps is right," said Papa. "Besides, if Two-Ton had stolen these parts, he would have sold them to a classic car collector by now."

"Right you are, Papa," said Gramps. "I think I know what must have happened. The thief didn't know how valuable these parts would become, so he sold them to Two-Ton for a few dollars. And Two-Ton didn't know how valuable they'd become, either, so he tossed them out on his lot with all the junk. And that's where they've been these many years!"

Chapter 6
The Great Car Robbery

The very same hood ornament and hubcaps that had been stolen from the Bear family roadster way back in 1955! It seemed too good to be true. But it *was* true. Gramps had proved it. And a great boon it was to Papa's chances of winning a prize at the big car show. Both Gramps and Papa had taken

good care of the red roadster over the years. It was in great condition. And now it had all its original parts.

The red roadster, with its shiny hood ornament and gleaming hubcaps, looked terrific as Papa drove it slowly up Main Street in the grand procession of classic cars on the day before the big show was to open. Just in front of Papa were three of Squire Grizzly's chauffeurs, driving the squire's 1938 Grizzillac, his 1932 Bearsenburg, and his 1927 Bearcedes. And in front of *them,* at the head of the procession, was Squire Grizzly himself, driving his prized 1922 Bear MW.

The Bear MW was a convertible, and the squire had the top down. Like many of the other owner-drivers, he wore a long white duster, the kind of coat drivers often wore to keep the dust off their clothes in the old days of open cars and dirt roads. Proudly, he, Papa, and the other owners drove their

classic cars onto the Bear Country School athletic field, which was decked with flags and bunting.

Bears from all over Bear Country were already pouring into Beartown for the big show. The state police were stationed along all the roads into Beartown to control the traffic. Beartown's hotels and motels were full. So were its shops and restaurants. It seemed as if the classic car show was just about the greatest event in Beartown history.

Until the big day came. That's when disaster struck.

Early that morning, before the athletic

field opened to the public, Barry Bruin showed Mayor Honeypot the podium that had been built for his opening speech.

"That will foo dust jine," said the mayor, who had a habit of getting the fronts and backs of his words mixed up. "Er, I mean, do just fine."

But Barry didn't hear the mayor. He was looking in horror across the sea of classic cars on the athletic field. "Oh, no!" he gasped. "I don't believe it!"

"Rut's wong?" asked the mayor. "I mean, what's wrong?"

"Cars are missing!" cried Barry. He counted, "...five, six, seven...*eight!*"

"Mars are kissing?" said the mayor. "I mean, cars are missing? That's terrible! Bet Chief Gruno! Er, get Chief Bruno!"

Barry dashed to the school building and called not only Chief of Police Bruno but also Squire Grizzly and Papa Bear. That's because the eight missing cars included Papa's red roadster and all four of the cars the squire had entered in the show.

Squire Grizzly and Papa Bear reached the athletic field even before Chief Bruno. Papa was out of breath because he'd run all the way from the tree house. But the squire, who had ridden in one of his chauffeured Grizzillacs, had plenty of breath. "Stolen!" he roared. "My four finest classic cars! This is an outrage!"

Papa just looked sadly out at the empty space where his red roadster had been. The

squire put an arm around his shoulders and said, "Cheer up, friend. You lost a car, but *I* lost *four*."

"But you must have twice as many cars in your collection," answered Papa.

"*Thrice* as many," the squire said proudly.

"I just lost my entire collection," Papa said. "Besides, my family has no way of getting around now."

Just then Mama and the cubs came running up. In his panic, Papa had run way ahead of them. Now they stood panting, staring at the spot where their car had been.

Squire Grizzly realized the Bears were in much worse shape than he was. He offered

to loan them a Grizzillac with a chauffeur. Papa and Mama accepted gratefully.

Then the squire turned to Chief Bruno, who had just arrived. "How will you catch these crooks?" he demanded.

Mayor Honeypot spoke up in support of his chief of police. "That'll be difficult, Squire," he said. "By now the thieves must be gong lawn. Er, I mean, long gone."

"Oh, no, they aren't," said the chief. "The state police have been watching all the roads out of town. And they have orders to stop any classic cars going out of Beartown until the car show is over."

"Maybe the thieves aren't outsiders," suggested Brother. "Maybe someone from Beartown did it."

"Yes, and I know who!" cried Squire Grizzly. "Ralph Ripoff! Once again that sleazy swindler has lived up to his name!"

Chief Bruno shook his head. "I don't think so, Squire," he said. "Ralph's just a small-time con artist. He could never pull off a multimillion-dollar car theft."

"But he might be involved," insisted the squire.

Chief Bruno frowned and scratched his head. He was in a tough spot. He and Officer Marguerite had their hands full with the car show. There was no way they could investigate a major crime at the same time.

"Okay, here's what I'll do," said the chief. "For today, I'll deputize the Bear Detectives to search Beartown for the stolen cars. They know the area as well as anybody. They can share the squire's loaner car. And I'll give them a police radio so they can contact me at any time."

Brother and Sister had been standing there with sad looks on their faces, thinking about their stolen car and how bad Papa and Mama must be feeling. But now their eyes lit up. Riding around in a chauffeured Grizzillac to investigate the Great Car Robbery! Cool!

"The Bear Detectives reporting for duty!" they chorused.

"Good," said Chief Bruno. "First, I want you to pay Ralph a visit and see what he knows. After that, check out all the places where the cars might be hidden: garages, warehouses, unused factories."

"Right, Chief," said Brother. "We'll go get Lizzy and Cousin Fred right away. And we'll make Barry an honorary Bear Detective for the day. His car knowledge might help us solve the case."

THE BEAR DETECTIVES REPORTING FOR DUTY!

Chapter 7
Searching for Clues

The Bear Detectives added Bonnie Brown to their group—that was Brother's idea, of course—and headed for Ralph Ripoff's houseboat. The chauffeur parked the limo at the edge of the woods, and the cubs went the rest of the way on foot.

When the cubs told Ralph about the Great Car Robbery, his eyes grew wide. "No kidding?" he said. "That's wonderful! Er...I mean, that's *terrible!*"

It was obvious that Ralph knew nothing about the robbery. When Brother told him that Squire Grizzly had suspected him, he smiled. "Why, that's a great compliment," he said. "Make sure you thank the good squire for me. But I could never pull off a big operation like that. I can only admire it from afar."

"That's what Chief Bruno said," Sister added.

Ralph looked a little hurt. "That doesn't surprise me," he muttered. "The chief never had any respect for my work."

"Well, thanks for your time," said Brother as the Bear Detectives left the houseboat. "Would you keep your ear to the ground and let us know if you hear anything?"

"Waste of time," said Ralph. "It's been my

experience that the only thing you get from keeping your ear to the ground is a dirty ear."

The Bear Detectives spent the rest of the day crisscrossing Beartown. Every time they found a likely spot to search, they parked the limo far away and walked the rest of the way to avoid suspicion. They searched every garage, warehouse, and abandoned factory they could find. But not a single stolen car turned up.

Finally, after their last warehouse search on the outskirts of town, they headed for home. Brother radioed Chief Bruno from the limo and told him that their search had failed. Just as Brother switched off the radio, Barry pointed to an open field and cried, "Stop the car!"

"What is it?" asked Brother.

"That old, empty barn over there in the

field," said Barry. "We haven't searched it yet."

"You go, Barry," said Brother. "I'm tired." So was everyone else.

The cubs watched Barry cross the field and disappear into the barn. Moments later, he came out and started walking back to the car. As he crossed a dirt road that ran past the barn, he stopped in his tracks. He bent over and looked at something in the road. Then he waved excitedly. The cubs hopped from the car and ran to him.

"Look!" Barry said, pointing at the muddy road.

"Tire tracks," said Cousin Fred. "So what? They could have been made by any one of hundreds of cars."

"Oh, no, they couldn't!" said Barry. "The pattern of the tread is from a classic car. The cars in the show all have custom-made tires that look exactly like the original tires!"

"Gee, that's right!" said Brother. "Papa's almost didn't get made in time for the show. All he talked about the last few days were those stupid tires."

Barry dashed to the limo and came back with a thick book. "With this I can pinpoint the exact make of the car that made these tracks," he said.

Sister leaned over to look at the book's title and did a double-take. *"Tires of the World?"* she said. "Are you kidding?

There's a whole book about *tires?*"

Barry just stared at her. "Are *you* kidding?" he said. "This is only the first volume of five!"

"Well that speaks *volumes* about you car nuts," muttered Sister.

But the others were thankful for Barry's passion for cars. Within seconds, he had determined that the tracks were from a 1927 Bearcedes touring car.

"Wow," said Cousin Fred. "I guess that proves it. Where do you think this road goes?"

Brother looked off down the road. "Out toward Birder's Woods," he said. "I can see it in the distance."

"Maybe the classic cars are hidden in Birder's Woods!" said Sister.

"Only one way to find out," said Bonnie. "Let's follow the tracks."

After Brother told the chauffeur to wait in the Nature Walk parking lot at Birder's Woods, the Bear Detectives followed the Bearcedes tracks. But the tracks didn't go into Birder's Woods, after all. They went around *behind* Birder's Woods and wound up at...

"Parts R Us," said Sister, reading the sign on the locked gate that stood before them.

"This dirt road goes to the back gate of Two-Ton's auto graveyard!" said Cousin Fred.

"It's the perfect place to hide stolen cars," said Barry. "You could dirty them up and put them out there with all those wrecks. No one would ever know."

"But why is there only one set of tracks?" Sister wondered. *"Eight* classic cars were stolen."

But Barry had already found more tracks. He was bending down, hands on knees, examining them. "Classic, classic, classic...," he said. "A whole bunch of tracks!"

"Look!" said Lizzy. "There's another dirt road that joins this one!" She pointed into the distance. "It goes off toward town. The other cars must have been brought in that way."

"I'll bet they're all in there," said Brother, pointing beyond the gate. "And I know who put them there."

"Who?" asked Barry.

"Two-Ton Grizzly, of course," said Brother. "He's a car thief, for sure. I suspected him of being a thief last week, but Papa and Gramps talked me out of it."

"Why did you suspect Two-Ton of being a thief?" asked Lizzy.

"Tell you later," said Brother. "We don't have any time to waste now."

"Why?" said Sister. "What are we going to do?"

"Climb the fence and search," said Brother.

Sister shivered. "You mean we have to go into the *auto graveyard?*" she gasped. "But it's almost dark..."

"Come on, Sis," said Brother. "It's not a real graveyard."

Sister thought hard. Finally, in a voice that was almost a whisper, she said, "Okay...I guess."

Chapter 8
Ghosts?

It didn't take the Bear Detectives long to locate some of the stolen cars. Four of them, including Squire Grizzly's 1932 Bearsenburg and 1938 Grizzillac, were hidden not far from the back gate, amid piles of spare parts. But none of the other stolen cars were anywhere to be found.

Barry sat on a rusty old crankcase, shaking his head. "I can't understand it," he said. "Where are the other four?"

"Maybe the thieves moved them some-where else in town," suggested Lizzy.

"What for?" said Brother. "This is the perfect hiding place."

"Or took them out of town already," added Sister.

"How?" said Cousin Fred. "The state police are watching all the roads. Remember, we're talking about cars, not airplanes."

"Well," said Brother, "at least we know who the crooks are now."

You might think the cubs would be happy about solving the case. But they weren't.

"It's too bad about Two-Ton," said Brother glumly.

"Yeah," said Bonnie. "And Too-Tall, Too-Much, and Too-Too. I'll bet they were in on it."

Sister shook her head sadly. "And we always thought Too-Tall was the only bad

apple in the family barrel," she said. "And even *he* wasn't all bad. Sometimes I even sort of liked the big guy." She looked around the darkening lot and shivered again. It was already dusk. "Let's get out of here," she said. "It's starting to get spooky."

Just then the cubs let out a collective gasp. A flashlight was shining at them through the windows of a wrecked car.

"What are you creeps doing here?" It was Too-Tall's voice. The flashlight beam shifted to a nearby sign that read TRESPASSERS WILL BE PROSECUTED. "Can't you read?"

"We can read, all right," said Brother bravely. He pointed to the 1932 Bearsenburg. "But car thieves will be prosecuted, too!"

Too-Tall stepped out from behind the wrecked car and stared at the Bearsenburg. His eyes were as big as saucers. "You mean...you think my dad...is a car thief?" he stammered.

"Not just your dad!" said Brother. "Your mom, your sister...and *you,* too!"

"What?" gasped Too-Tall. "You can't be

YOU MEAN... YOU THINK MY DAD... IS A CAR THIEF?

serious! If you don't take that back, I'm gonna clean up the graveyard *with you!*" He looked mad enough to do it, too.

"I don't think he's acting, guys," Bonnie told the others.

"How can you tell?" asked Barry.

"Don't you remember him in the school play last year?" said Bonnie. "He's not that good an actor."

"Oh, yeah?" snarled Too-Tall. "If you don't clear out of here, I'm gonna show you just how *bad* an actor I can be!"

"Oh, yeah yourself, you big goon!" said Brother. "We're gonna go get Chief Bruno and—"

"No, wait!" said Fred. "Bonnie might be right."

"Then what about the stolen hood ornament and hubcaps Bonnie and I found here?" said Brother.

"Those?" said Barry. "If Two-Ton had stolen those, he would have gotten rid of them by now."

Cousin Fred and Bonnie both agreed with Barry. That made Brother pause to think. Five different bears, including Gramps and Papa, had now said exactly the same thing about the stolen parts. Maybe he was wrong about Two-Ton and his family, after all. But there was one last bit of evidence that still bothered him.

"Then what about this?" said Brother. "When Bonnie and I were here earlier this week, Two-Ton said that he didn't like to be on the lot at night because he has poor night vision. But it was obvious he could see just fine. I thought it was a fishy story at the time. Now it seems even fishier. Like he was trying to set us up."

"Set us up?" said Bonnie. "For what?"

"For thinking that he couldn't be the classic car thief," said Brother. "He *knew* the Great Car Robbery would happen at night!"

Too-Tall just stared at Brother for a moment. Then he leaned close and said, "Don't you ever let on I told you this. But you've got it all wrong."

"Then why did he make up that phony story about night vision?" said Brother. "He zipped through this lot at dusk like a cat after a mouse!"

"Because," said Too-Tall, lowering his voice to a near whisper, *"he's afraid of the dark."*

"Afraid of the dark?" said Brother. "Your dad? The biggest, strongest bear in Bear Country?"

"Yeah," said Too-Tall. "That's why he was in such a hurry to get back to the office at dusk. He goes all to pieces in the dark. To cover it up, he tells folks he's got poor night vision. And if you ever tell anybody I said so, you're dead meat!"

Too-Tall seemed to relax a little. Was that because he thought he was fooling them? wondered Brother.

"He even sleeps with the dashboard lights on, you know," Too-Tall went on. "But you shoulda seen him last night. He was really in top form. He woke up in the middle of the night, looked out of his bedroom windshield, and thought he saw a *ghost!*"

"Gh-gh-ghost?" said Sister.

"He said it was floating among the wrecked cars," said Too-Tall. Then he leaned down toward Sister and shined the flashlight up at his own face. He grinned a wicked grin and hissed, *The Ghost of the Auto Graveyard*...BOO!"

Sister shrieked and hid behind Brother.

"How do we know you're not making this whole thing up?" said Brother.

"Hold on, Brother," said Fred. "Give the big guy a chance." He turned to Too-Tall. "Did this so-called ghost do anything besides float around?"

"Who knows?" said Too-Tall. "Pop ran to

wake up the rest of us as soon as he saw it. When we looked out our windows, guess what? There wasn't any ghost! Pure imagination."

"*Pure* imagination?" said Bonnie, frowning. "I wonder...Four of the stolen cars aren't here anymore. The thieves must have taken them out last night. If Too-Tall's telling the truth, maybe Two-Ton saw one of them and his imagination turned him into a ghost."

"Hmm," said Brother. "If that's true, the crooks might come back tonight for the rest of the cars. But I'm still not sure I believe Too-Tall. I've heard him tell too many lies in my time. I'd better radio Chief Bruno and let him deal with it."

"No!" said Too-Tall. "Don't do that! The chief'll come out here and question us Grizzlys till we're blue in the face. Maybe he

won't believe us...maybe he'll even *arrest* us! It'll be in all the newspapers! And by the time the real crooks get caught, my dad's business will be ruined!"

The cubs had never seen Too-Tall plead with anyone before. It shocked them. None of them knew what to believe now.

"So what do you suggest we do?" Brother asked Too-Tall.

"I'll tell you what, guys," said the gang leader. "You can all sleep over at my house tonight so you can keep an eye on our lot. I won't even tell my folks and sister that you found stolen cars here. If they're really the crooks, they'll try to take the rest of the stolen cars out of the lot when they think we're all asleep. And you'll see them do it."

"But how will we see them in the dark?" wondered Sister.

"My mom has a special pair of infrared binoculars," said Too-Tall. "She uses them to check out the lot whenever there's a noise at night. They'll be perfect for keeping watch. You can watch from my bedroom and make sure I don't sneak out to talk with the others. Well, what do you say? Will you do it?"

The Bear Detectives huddled. None of them liked the idea of not reporting the stolen cars to the chief. But Too-Tall seemed so desperate to prove his family's innocence that they just couldn't bring themselves to turn him down.

Chapter 9
The Haunted Graveyard

The cubs phoned their parents right away. Since they didn't say anything about watching for car thieves, it was easy to get permission to sleep over at Too-Tall's. All their parents were pleased. "I'm so glad you're getting along with Too-Tall for a change" was Mama Bear's response. Then Two-Ton called Squire Grizzly, who phoned the chauffeur of the cubs' limo and told him to pick the cubs up in the morning.

From Too-Tall's bedroom windshield, the Bear Detectives watched the auto graveyard in shifts. Sister, Lizzy, and Barry kept watch first. At midnight, they were replaced by Brother, Bonnie, and Cousin Fred. The moon cast a pale glow over the lot. For hours the trio saw nothing but the dim shapes of old cars and heaps of spare parts. It was a ghostly sight, but without any ghosts.

By three in the morning, the cubs' eyelids were starting to feel heavy. But then something happened that snapped them wide open again.

"Look!" said Bonnie. "Out by the back gate! It looks like a *ghost!*"

From a distance, the figure seemed to float among the wrecked cars. Sure enough, it looked like a white-sheeted ghost!

"You're right!" said Brother. "And I see

another one! *Two* ghosts! I can't believe it! The auto graveyard *is* haunted!"

Cousin Fred trained the infrared binoculars on the pair of ghostly figures. "I've got news for you," he said. "Those aren't ghosts. They only look like ghosts because they're wearing long white dusters."

"Like the ones some of the drivers wore in the classic car procession?" said Bonnie.

Fred nodded. "They may not be ghosts," he said, "but they definitely *are* car thieves! They're each getting into a stolen car."

The cubs heard the sound of car engines starting in the distance.

"Now they're driving the cars out the back gate," said Fred. "They must have picked the lock."

"Who are they?" asked Bonnie.

Fred lowered the binoculars. "Sorry, guys," he said. "I couldn't get a good look at their faces. But they're coming back later for the other two cars."

"How do you know?" asked Brother.

"Elementary, my dear Brother," said Fred, pretending to be his favorite detective, the famous Bearlock Holmes. "They left the back gate wide open."

Chapter 10
Down a Lazy River

The Bear Detectives woke up Too-Tall and told him what had happened. Immediately, he woke up his parents and sister. Brother radioed Chief Bruno while Too-Too and Too-Much got ready to nab the thieves when they returned.

But what if the thieves didn't return? Brother pointed out that they might have left the back gate open by accident. So he grabbed a flashlight and set out with Bonnie and Barry to track the stolen cars. They followed the fresh tire tracks along the back road that led past the old abandoned barn. Soon the road veered away from the main highway toward Old Grizzly River.

"Where does this dirt road go, anyway?" wondered Bonnie.

"I'm not sure," said Brother. "But if it follows Old Grizzly River, it'll go through the woods and right by Ralph Ripoff's houseboat."

"Does that mean *Ralph* is the head thief?" gasped Bonnie.

"We'll know when we get there," said Brother. "Come on! Faster!"

Meanwhile, back at Parts R Us, two more "ghosts" had already appeared.

"Look!" said Sister. "They're sneaking through the back gate!"

"How could they get back so soon?" wondered Lizzy.

"There must be *four* thieves in all," said Cousin Fred.

"YIKES!" cried Sister as two strange-looking creatures joined them at the windshield.

"Don't be alarmed!" said Too-Too. "It's just me and Too-Much wearing infrared goggles—our thief-chasin' goggles! There they are, Too-Much! Let's nab those creeps!"

The goggled bears rushed out into the night. "Hey, wait for me!" yelled Too-Tall, stumbling after them without goggles or flashlight.

Sister, Lizzy, and Cousin Fred wrestled over the binoculars. Fred, being the strongest, won. In an instant, he had trained them on the "ghosts." "Wow!" he said. "Too-Too just tackled one of them around the legs! And Too-Much just grabbed them

both by their collars and knocked their
heads together! Looks as if they're out
cold!"

"What about Too-Tall?" asked Sister.

Fred scanned the lot. "He's off by himself, staggering around in the dark. I think
he's lost."

Just then sirens were heard from the

direction of the front gate.

"Here come the chief and Officer Marguerite," said Fred. "Let's go meet them."

Meanwhile, the other Bear Detectives were deep in the woods, following the dirt road along Old Grizzly River. As they neared Ralph Ripoff's place, Bonnie pointed downriver. "There's the houseboat," she said. "I can see it in the moonlight. And two cars are on the deck!"

"My eyes must be playing tricks on me," said Barry. "It looks like it's shrinking."

"That's because it's *moving away!*" said Brother.

The cubs hurried to the spot on the river-bank where the houseboat had been moored. The boat was already downriver at least a hundred yards.

"Hey, Ralph!" yelled the cubs. "Come back here!"

But the darkened houseboat just glided down the lazy river in the early morning moonlight.

The Bear Detectives flopped down in the grass. They were exhausted.

"So *that's* how he's been getting the stolen cars out of town," said Bonnie. "On his houseboat!"

"No wonder the state police guarding the roads never saw anything," said Barry.

Brother shook his head. "It's hard to believe," he said. "Ralph, a small-time swindler, pulling off a multimillion-dollar car theft. If I hadn't seen it with my own eyes—"

Just then, as if in answer, a muffled voice was heard.

"What was that?" said Bonnie.

"*Grmpff! Grmpff!*" said the voice.

"I know what that is!" said Brother. "It's a bear bound and gagged! And it's coming from the reeds on the riverbank!"

The cubs rushed to the sound of the voice. There among the tall reeds, with his hands and feet tied and a rag stuffed into his mouth, lay Ralph Ripoff.

"Wow!" said Barry. "Ralph's pretty darn smart! He stole the cars, then tied himself up to make it look as if he didn't do it!"

Brother and Bonnie just stared at Barry in amazement.

"If Ralph's pretty darn smart," said Brother, "then you're a regular genius, Barry. Come on, let's untie him."

"Squawk!" cried Ralph the moment the gag was out of his mouth.

"He's forgotten how to speak!" gasped Barry.

"You ninny!" snapped Ralph. "I'm talking about my parrot! Are you all right, my little pet?" He reached behind him and held up his pet parrot, Squawk, who was also bound and gagged. "Don't worry, little fella! I'll set you free!"

Squawk had been quiet all tied up, but as soon as he could open his beak, he let out a stream of shrieks. "Help!" he squawked. "Help! Stop, thief! STOP, THIEF!"

"Shut up, birdbrain!" barked Ralph. "It's all over now!"

"Who did it, Ralph?" asked Brother. "Who tied you up and took your house-boat?"

Ralph's face twisted into a grimace. "Captain Billy and Otto," he muttered.

"You mean the crooks who tried to swindle Dr. Gert Grizzly out of money for the new hospital wing?" said Bonnie.

HELP! STOP, THIEF! STOP, THIEF!

"And threw you into Great Roaring River?" added Barry.

"That's right," said Ralph. "The former owner and strongman of Captain Billy's Colossal Circus and Carnival. They just loaded two cars on the houseboat and took off. Did the same thing twice last night. Apparently, trying to drown me last summer wasn't enough for them. They had to come back and torment me some more. I've been lying here all tied up for over twenty-four hours!"

"But I thought Captain Billy and Otto were in Bear Country Prison," said Brother.

"You and everyone else," said Ralph bitterly.

Well, not *everyone*. When Brother, Bonnie, Barry, and Ralph joined the rest of the Bear Detectives at the police station, they found that Chief Bruno had suspected Captain Billy and Otto from the beginning.

"A couple of days before the car show," said the chief, "the state police called all us local chiefs to tell us that Billy and Otto had escaped from prison." He pointed to a jail cell, where two bears in white dusters stood glowering at him. "These two jokers escaped with them. Shifty Sheldon and Clarence the Crook. They all must have sneaked into Beartown disguised as classic car owners. But now these creeps are headed straight back to Bear Country

Prison. And in a few minutes so will Captain Billy and Otto."

Chief Bruno picked up the phone and punched in a number. "Hello, river police? Bruno here. I've got two of the classic car thieves in my jail cell. The other two are headed down Old Grizzly River in Ralph Ripoff's houseboat. Nab 'em!"

Chapter 11
Recovering the Loot

It was dawn when the river police called Chief Bruno to report that they had captured Captain Billy and Otto. The chief immediately phoned Squire Grizzly, Papa Bear, and the other owners of the stolen cars to tell them the good news. Within minutes, Papa and the squire reached the police station, both in chauffeured Grizzillacs.

"Any news about my cars, Chief?" asked

Squire Grizzly eagerly.

"And mine?" asked Papa.

"We found the '32 Bearsenburg and '38 Grizzillac at Parts R Us," said Chief Bruno. "But so far there's no news about the '27 Bearcedes or the '22 Bear MW. Or your red roadster, either, Papa."

All the air seemed to go out of Papa and the squire.

The chief turned to Ralph and said, "But your houseboat is being brought back up Old Grizzly River right this minute."

Ralph's eyes twinkled. "Well, I hope you get your cars back, gentlemen," he said to Papa and the squire. Then he turned and tipped his straw hat to the bears in the jail cell. "And I hope *you* two have a pleasant trip *up the river!* Toodle-oo!" And with a twirl of his cane, he was out the door.

Just then the phone rang. Chief Bruno

answered, "Bruno here...Yes...That's great...
I'll tell them."

"Our cars?" said Papa and the squire in
unison.

"Right," said the chief with a smile. "The
Big Bear City police just found them in an
abandoned warehouse on Great Roaring
River, not far from where Old Grizzly River
feeds into it. And they're all in perfect condition."

"Hooray!" shouted the Bear Detectives.
Papa and the squire locked arms and did a
little victory dance right there in the police
station.

Chapter 12
Collector's Dreams

The Big Bear City police brought the stolen cars back just in time for their owners to enter them in the big show before the final judging. To no one's surprise, Squire Grizzly's 1922 Bear MW won first prize and his 1927 Bearcedes won second prize. To everyone's surprise but Papa Bear's, third prize was awarded to the Bear family's shiny red GG roadster. Most bears weren't aware of the history of the 1954 model. But the judges, who were all from the Classic Car and Truck Museum in Big Bear City, knew that only a handful of the '54 roadsters had been made before Grizzly Garage went out of business. And as far as anyone knew, the Bear family's roadster was the *only one* left in all Bear Country! That made it even more valuable than many of the much older antique cars in the show.

By the end of the afternoon, it became clear to everyone that the classic car show had been a huge success despite the Great Car Robbery. It had raised a carload of

money for Bear Country School.

After Mayor Honeypot gave the closing speech, the Bear family crowded around Papa to admire the prize he'd won. It was a beautiful silver loving cup.

Meanwhile, Squire Grizzly wasn't even looking at his own prizes. Instead, he was greedily eyeing Papa's prize. First prize and second prize weren't enough for him. He

had expected to win all three. And the squire was a bear who was used to getting his way.

The squire pushed his way through the crowd and approached Papa. "Well, friend," he said with a big smile, "you stole—er, I mean, won—third prize fair and square. I had no idea yours was the only 1954 GG roadster left in Bear Country. Would you consider selling it?"

For just a moment, Papa got a far-off look in his eye. Perhaps he was thinking of all the money his red roadster would bring. "I'm afraid not," he told Squire Grizzly. "After all, this car is my entire collection."

"Oh, yes, I forgot," said the squire. "You're a collector now, aren't you?"

"Sure am," said Papa, beaming. "In fact, I've been thinking of looking for another classic car to add to my collection."

Mama and the cubs looked at Papa as if he'd gone crazy.

"Well," said Squire Grizzly, "if that's the case, I just might be willing to part with my 1946 Grizzillac sedan."

"You would?" said Papa.

"And since you're such a good friend, I'll sell it to you cheap," said the squire. "How does a million dollars sound?"

Papa swooned. Mama and the cubs had

to hold him up as his knees buckled. He made a loud gulping noise and tried to catch his breath.

"Are you all right?" asked Squire Grizzly.

"Oh...er, uh...sure," mumbled Papa. "Come to think of it, Squire, we don't really have room in the driveway for another car..."

Nodding in agreement, Mama and the cubs led Papa quickly to the red roadster. It was high time to head for home.

Stan and Jan Berenstain began writing and illustrating books for children in the early 1960s, when their two young sons were beginning to read. That marked the start of the best-selling Berenstain Bears series. Now, with more than one hundred books in print, videos, television shows, and even Berenstain Bears attractions at major amusement parks, it's hard to tell where the Bears end and the Berenstains begin!

Stan and Jan make their home in Bucks County, Pennsylvania, near their sons— Leo, a writer, and Michael, an illustrator— who are helping them with Big Chapter Books stories and pictures. They plan on writing and illustrating many more books for children, especially for their four grand-children, who keep them well in touch with the kids of today.